Quantum Lace

~ BOOK THREE ~

Quantum Lace

Book Three

Dedicated to Mr Ken Burns and his incredible team from whom I learned more about – and was more profoundly affected by – the human stories of the Civil War than I ever expected

...and to our dear departed Mr Shelby Foote whose stories and perspectives gave me an entirely different understanding of what it meant – and means – to be a 'Southerner'.

Requests for permission to reproduce parts of this work should be addressed to the author.
Contact information can be found here:

www.QuantumLace.com

If you would like to invite the author to speak at an event for your organization, please contact Leigh (Bella) St John via the website.

The contents of this book are the intellectual property of the author, who deserves to be compensated for the time and energy invested in this work.

Copyright © 2017 Leigh St John aka Bella St John

Thank you and I hope you enjoy the book...

---

www.QuantumLace.com

Prologue

While you can read this book as a stand-alone short story, it is preferable if you first read Book One where you not only learn how Lady Bridgit Darnell travelled from Victorian England in 1895 and ultimately came to be in the predicament in which she finds herself at the beginning of this book, but also the background information and science behind how she is able to time travel – and why she chose to do so in the first place...

Links to Book One on Amazon:
US Customers:
http://bit.ly/quantumlace
UK Customers:
http://bit.ly/quantumlace-uk

Introduction

This story of time-travel you are about to read, while a work of fiction, is largely based on real science, real people and real events. Where fact leaves off and fiction begins is for you to decide.

Read the first chapter of Book One for free here (www.QuantumLace.com) where you will learn the quantum physics behind how Bridgit is able to travel through time...

...and do a search on just about anything mentioned in this book – or any book in the Quantum Lace series – and then make up your own mind what is 'real'...

Table of Contents

Prologue 3

Introduction 4

Chapter One 6

Chapter Two – Memories? 16

Chapter Three – What does it mean to be 'Free'? 30

Chapter Four – Dinner with the Enemy 44

Chapter Five – The Flag is Raised 56

Chapter Six – Reconciliation Dinner 66

Chapter Seven – Martyrs of the Race Course 88

...and then... 99

Acknowledgements 103

Thank you... 107

About the Author 109

www.QuantumLace.com

Chapter One

"Are y'all right, ma'am?" Bridgit heard a deep male voice ask in a slow drawl.

As she opened her eyes, Bridgit saw a young woman beside her fussing about, waving a handkerchief in Bridgit's face, and a tall figure of a man that seemed so large and impressive as to obliterate the entire view.

"She fainted when she heard about General Lee's surrender," cried the woman in a high-pitched drawl To Bridgit's ears it sounded like, "She fAYinted when she hAYrd about General LAYs surrAYnder."

News of the surrender by Confederate General Robert E. Lee at Appomattox Court House on April 9th, 1865 took only three days to travel to Charleston, South Carolina; the southern state at the genesis of the conflict.

The American Civil War had been decimating the country, and its various ways of life for four years – and slaughtering primarily its young male population to the tune of approximately eighteen dead soldiers every single hour, after hour, after hour, after hour... Twenty-four hours per day, every day after day after day, 365 days per year... For four long, soul-destroying years...

The deaths were not the only toll on human life. In the coming months, a full one-fifth of Mississippi's entire state budget would be spent on artificial limbs...

"Cap, help her over here to sit down," said the young woman and motioned to a pile of bricks that looked as though they had once been part of a fence belonging to a house that no longer existed.

Despite his size, the mountain of a man carefully but deftly assisted Bridgit to the makeshift seat before retreating several paces.

"I was so worried when you collapsed like that when I told you the awful news," said the woman, rather hysterically and in a voice that sounded comical and overly-accentuated, "and I am so glad Cap was here to fetch you off the ground because, Lord knows, I just didn't know what else to do with you feinting like that! What else was I supposed to do?"

Bridgit held up her hand in an attempt to stop the high-pitched tirade.

"I am fine. Really, I am," Bridgit replied as she regained her composure and looked about at the peculiar mingling of beautiful buildings, mounds of rubble, and house-less chimneys standing to attention against the late-afternoon sky.

At least when she drew her attention to her clothing, there was something comforting and familiar about the fact that she was wearing a corset, even though her skirt was so large as to be ridiculous.

"I just *can't* believe you would go out *alone*," screeched the woman – with Bridgit's ears almost hurting as she heard "KAYnt" in a tone better suited to the ears of a canine – "and make me come out here with Cap looking for you! Lord knows what might have happened to me!"

Deciding the course of action that would lead to the least chattering would be to simply say, "let's go," Bridgit did just that, brushed off her balloon of a skirt and proceeded to follow the other woman, with the large man following several steps behind.

As they walked to their destination, Bridgit was interested to note that they passed several uniformed soldiers along the way, and each – without even one exception – was dark-skinned. Not one bore any resemblance to the uniforms worn by Jack's brother and his compatriots... and this was definitely not Hastings.

Arriving at a beautiful three-storey home that appeared surprisingly undamaged in comparison to many others they had passed, Bridgit and the woman walked in through the massive front door, while the man disappeared around the side of the building.

"Minnie, get us some lemonade," the young woman ordered a tall, slender dark-skinned servant in her thirties as Bridgit walked through the door.

"Miss, ya know we don't have any lemons but I can fix y'all some tall glasses of water."

Dismissing the servant with an indifferent flip of her hand, the young woman sat on an elegant sofa in the front parlour and patted the seat next to her, encouraging Bridgit to sit; as Bridgit smiled an apology to the servant.

Bridgit surveyed the room. It was like looking at a jigsaw puzzle that had pieces missing. An empty space above the mantle where once would have hung a painting or mirror... An intricately carved stand beside the window that once would have supported a fine statue, now standing without purpose... Broad windows whose vista would have been framed by curtains draped in stylised folds and whose glass would once have shone without a blemish, now naked and unadorned with glass so grubby one needed to concentrate and squint to make out the view beyond... Magnificent wide oak floorboards that would once have borne expensive woven carpets now lay bare and barren and did nothing to muffle the sound of Bridgit's shoes. The whole room echoed her steps as she approached the sofa.

"Now, tell me, what possessed you to go walking about by yourself like that?" demanded the young, attractive blonde woman who appeared to be no more than twenty-three at most.

Bridgit sat for a moment, not sure what to say, but eventually responded tentatively with, "perhaps you could start by telling me where I am?"

"What do you mean, 'where are you'? Why, you're in Father's house here in Charleston, you silly squirrel!"

In Bridgit's mind, the last thing she remembered was going to sleep in the south of England during the second World War, wishing she was back in her own time, and thinking about Charles – Dr Charles Preston – and the posy ring he had given her at 'home' in 1895. "When this ye see, remember me".

Then the word hit her – Charleston! The same place she met Markus and began this rabbit-hole journey – but this was definitely not the same period in time...

Noticing an absent expression on Bridgit's face, the young woman quizzically asked, "well, if you don't know where you are, what DO you remember?"

Bridgit sat thinking...

"But, Charlotte! You just must remember *me*!" The squeal interrupted Bridgit's thoughts... "I'm Betty-Sue! You must remember me!" The young woman's already capacious blue eyes were opened even wider, and her pale skin was taking on a tone of flushed pinkish-red.

Feeling an overwhelmingly present urge to calm the young woman, who seemed more a child than a fully-grown adult, she took the girl's hand and patted it. Bridgit still was far from accustomed at turning up in different times and different places, not knowing initially where or 'when' she was, but she knew enough to play along until she could find her footing... and now she also realized her name here was not Bridgit, but Charlotte.

"I am sure I remember you," she replied soothingly. "Just give me a moment."

Chapter Two - Memories?

As Bridgit sat next to the anxious girl, she wondered what on earth she could say to mitigate the fact that she had no idea where she was, nor who 'Betty-Sue' was...

But then, as she pondered the situation, Bridgit began to recall images and details that felt like memories – but couldn't possibly be... Could they? Bridgit knew for certain she had not experienced the visions that were beginning to flood into her mind... Or had she?

"A fire..." said Bridgit absently as she searched her mind for some context to these images. "I remember a fire."

"Yes! That's right," said Betty-Sue, urging Bridgit on.

Bridgit sat silent for the longest period, occasionally shaking her head as if to unrattled the bizarre collective of visions. "The clouds of smoke... It felt like the fire would consume everything..." thought Bridgit aloud.

"That's right!" responded a gleeful Betty-Sue, "and if it hadn't been for our glorious General Lee staying at the Mills House, the fire might well have continued this direction."

Bumped out of her ruminations by this seemingly nonsensical statement, Bridgit asked, "What do you mean?"

"Why, the wind change, of course!" replied Betty-Sue in a rather demeaning tone.

Bridgit's perplexed look was enough to prompt the girl to continue; although Betty Sue sighed at the exasperating thought of having to explain herself.

"General Lee was staying at the Mills House and they were all up on the roof watching the fire approach but, just at the last minute, the wind changed direction. We all know it was because the General was staying there. He's blessed, you know!" crowed Betty-Sue.

Now too far in not to learn the rest, Bridgit braced herself and asked, "Blessed?"

"Why yeeeeeeees!" responded Betty-Sue, with the words almost dripping off her lips as she sensed an opportunity to be the star of this recitation.

"Did you know that his mother died more than a year before he was born?" said Betty-Sue more as a statement than a question.

Not having had children herself but knowing that the gestation of a human is, give or take, nine months, Bridgit hesitantly asked Betty-Sue to continue with her explanation.

Delighted at the unusual request of actually being *asked* to continue, Betty-Sue said, "Well…….. His mother, Mrs Lee, you know, well, she was always sickly and this here one day she up and died – well, that's what everyone thought!" Betty-Sue was dragging this out like a good vaudevillian actor.

"She was put in a casket and three days later, the casket was put in the family vault – but," Betty-Sue paused for dramatic effect, "the story didn't end there..."

Bridgit had read her share of horror stories, preferred fact to fiction, and wasn't sure she desired to hear where this story would end up, but she motioned for her 'friend' to continue – as if she could have stopped her at this point even if she had wanted to.

"Well......." Again, with the dramatic pause. "The sexton was sweeping up the vault – a lot of people had been leaving flowers you know and he was sweeping up the petals and leaves and everything – and Mrs Lee started talking to him – from within her casket!"

Bridgit wasn't sure what to make of the story, but simply nodded her approval for its continuation.

"Well, that's just it! She wasn't dead!" squealed Betty-Sue. "It was more than a year later that our General Robert E. Lee was born, so if that doesn't tell you that he's special, I don't know what will!"

Satisfied that even if it was irrational, Betty-Sue believed the tale - although later Bridgit was to learn every detail in the seemingly fanciful tale was true - Bridgit went back to not only wondering how she could have memories of something that she was certain she did not experience, but how that all related to her now sitting in the parlour of Betty-Sue's father's house.

"What do you remember since then?" quizzed Betty-Sue. "You must remember when those horrid black folk marched into our beloved Charleston like they owned the place, all dressed up in uniforms like they were something special?"

Betty-Sue was referring to February 21st, 1865 when the black 55th Massachusetts Infantry Regiment and 21st United States Coloured Infantry regiments (the latter included former slaves from the South Carolina Low Country, an area within close proximity to Charleston) marched into the city, three days after it had been captured.

While Bridgit didn't share Betty-Sue's obvious disgust at the black troops, the comment did spark a memory in her mind.

"I do remember a huge march of dark-skinned people," said Bridgit, still not sure how or why she was remembering things she knew she hadn't experienced.

"Ooooooh, yes," squirmed Betty-Sue. "First there were those black soldiers marching in, and then the rest of them thought they could just do what they please..."

"But these weren't soldiers," said Bridgit, still lost in thought, "and who is Jeff Davis? I know his name sounds familiar but I just cannot place him."

"Who is Jeff Davis?" Betty-Sue's incredulous high-pitched response was matched by her elevated volume.

"They were singing about Jeff Davis," recalled Bridgit. "All the children – there were hundreds and hundreds of them – all singing, "We'll hang Jeff Davis on a sour apple tree!""

"It was sooooooo disgusting!" Betty-Sue almost spat the words.

"...and there was a man on a cart auctioning a woman for sale as a cook?" Bridgit could hardly believe what she was recalling, "...and then fifty men or more tied to a rope behind the cart..."

"Oh, don't get flustered," said Betty-Sue with indignation. "They were all trying to make a point. They weren't really selling her off. It was all a joke at our expense," responded Betty-Sue with obvious condemnation.

"I don't understand," said Bridgit.

Betty-Sue proceeded to fill in the gaps for Bridgit around her memories of the black procession of around 10,000 now 'free' individuals through Charleston on March 29th, 1865 – a procession Bridgit recalled in part, but was sure she had not actually witnessed. After all, this was 1865 and, being born in December of 1864 in England, Bridgit would have been less than one-year old and on the other side of the world! But the fact was she *did* remember them... As Betty-Sue provided additional details, Bridgit recalled learning in history lessons the yet-to-happen fate of Jefferson Davis, the Confederate leader who did not hang from a sour apple tree, but rather spent 720 days in prison after the war, much of this time in a dungeon that was cold and damp, sleeping in a bug-infested bed, being forced to use a horse-bucket for water, and forbidden to see his wife for over a year.

Bridgit could not understand why she remembered both learning about this in her history lessons, and also actually *being there* – well, for some of it...

"They even had the impudence to have a coffin in the parade with the words, "Slavery is dead... Sumter dug his grave on the 13th of April, 1861!" Betty-Sue's continued rant brought Bridgit back from her thoughts to the conversation at hand, and left her wishing she could find some way to silence her young friend's outburst.

Thankfully and almost on cue, Minnie returned with their water.

"Thank you," said Bridgit as she took the glass - and received a glare from Betty-Sue.

"Y'all very welcome, Ma'am," replied Minnie very pointedly toward Bridgit, glancing sideways at Betty-Sue before leaving the room.

"Well, we had better go upstairs and rest before the dinner party tonight," said Betty-Sue, putting down the glass without even having taken a sip.

Bridgit had no recollection of a forthcoming dinner party, but wishing to avoid any further opportunity for Betty-Sue to exercise her vocal chords, Bridgit took a mouthful of water, placed the glass on the side table and rose to follow her hostess.

Now alone in her room, and thankful for the assistance of Minnie who had helped her out of the gigantic skirt that seemed as wide as it was long, Bridgit sat on the edge of the bed and attempted to make sense of what had just transpired.

She recalled learning of the American Civil War and President Abraham Lincoln's Emancipation Proclamation that essentially abolished slavery when it took effect on January 1st, 1863. Her governess had explained how Queen Victoria's statement of neutrality in reference to the conflict caused issues both at home and abroad: British merchants angry that the Crown was not supporting their continued trade with America; the Confederacy upset that the previous and vital support of British shipyards and cotton merchants would be withdrawn; and the Union upset that Britain was not taking a stand against slavery in American as it had done by outlawing the institution throughout the Empire in 1833.

Lying back on the large four-posted bed, Bridgit drifted off to sleep with an eclectic cacophony of thoughts fighting for precedence in her mind.

As she slept, Bridgit dreamed of her last encounter with Dr Charles Preston. His every feature seemed more pronounced in her slumber; the deep brown of his eyes, the strength and masculine beauty of his refined hands and long fingers, the way his cheeks would indent when he was lost in thought or contemplating what to say next...

Chapter Three - What does it mean to be 'Free'?

"Excuse me, Ma'am." Minnie's voice seemed to come from Charles' lips, until Bridgit slowly opened her eyes to see the servant standing beside the door.

"It is time to dress for dinner, Ma'am," said Minnie as she entered the room with a dark blue gown draped over her arm.

"Minnie – I'm sorry, that is your name, isn't it? My memory has been a little challenging of late," said Bridgit.

"Yes, Ma'am," replied the servant as she laid out the dress and other paraphernalia.

"Minnie, please tell me if I am being imprudent or if you do not want to answer, but I am curious," started Bridgit.

"Curious about what, Ma'am?" Minnie wasn't sure what was coming, however she already felt that the conversation was perhaps not one in which she would like to participate.

"Are you a slave?"

The question stopped Minnie mid-stretch as she reached for an undergarment.

"What do you mean, Ma'am?" asked Minnie in an attempt to deflect the impending inquisition.

Sensing the woman's hesitancy, Bridgit uttered, "never mind. I'm sorry. I should not have asked."

Minnie thought for a moment and then with a sigh that brought her shoulders back down from around her ears replied, "We is none of us slaves no more, Ma'am."

"But the way Betty-Sue treats you and speaks to you... I just thought..." Bridgit allowed her question to trail off.

Minnie stood looking at the floorboards for some time before responding.

"Miss Betty-Sue's father was always good to us and when he had to leave he asked us to make sure she was all right and that we would do whatever it took to keep her safe until he was able to come home – and that's just what me and Cap does. The others left when they heard the news that they was free, but me and Cap – we don't have nowheres else to go so we stay here with Miss Betty-Sue."

"But, if you're *free*," Bridgit started to reply and was cut off.

"*Free*?" said Minnie replied incredulously and perhaps louder than she had intended. Realising her slip, Minnie took a breath and in a softer tone continued, "I'm sorry, Ma'am, but free don't mean nothin'"

Sensing she had crossed a line, Minnie became silent but Bridgit wanted to hear the woman's side of the story and encouraged her to continue.

"It's all right," said Bridgit, "whatever you say will not leave this room." With that, Bridgit sat on the edge of the bed and waited for Minnie to continue.

After a long pause, Minnie spoke, hesitantly at first, and then as though the flood gates on her lifetime of anguish, hostility, frustration and feelings of futility had finally been opened.

"You have no idea what it's like," she began, pausing and taking a deep breath.

"I was born a slave; my mother was a slave; her mother before her was a slave - but I don't know where any of them is or even if they is still alive. I was sold from my mother's breast when I was a youngin - but I still remember it. I remember holdin' on to my mother's skirt as theys ripped open her top so they could see her back to see if she'd been whipped. I remember how one of them holds her as another pushed his hands into her mouth to check her teeth the same ways you would check a horse. I remember being wrenched from her skirt and held aloft as they said one day I would be good, strong 'breeding stock'. I didn't know what that meant then," she paused, "but I found out."

Minnie looked at Bridgit to see if she had shocked her to the point where she should not continue, but Bridgit kept very straight-faced and simply said, "go on."

"Don't get me wrong, Ma'am. Some massers are better than others – and Miss Betty-Sue's father is one o' the better ones – but they're not all like him."

"But surely, you are no longer a slave and he is no longer your 'master'?" questioned Bridgit.

"The law says me and Cap ain't slaves, Ma'am, but the law don't mean nothin'," Minnie replied, again bringing Cap into the conversation as though he and Minnie were connected in ways other than merely working together. "So, we is free and we can do what we like and go where we like and no one can stop us - but how do we *live,* Ma'am? We ain't got no money, no home except for this here house, no food. The whites pretend to still be our masters and look at us like we're nothin', but truth is they is scared of us now."

"Scared of you?" Bridgit asked.

Minnie shook her head. "Not scared of any one of us, Ma'am, but scared we'll all band together and then who knows what might happen." Now on a roll, Minnie continued. "...and then there's the likes of Mrs Weston. She's black same as me, but she was already a 'free' black woman when all this fightin' started. She and her mulatto husband owns more than ten slaves - well, they did own them," Minnie paused, "but even if those 'free' slaves wanted to stay on there, the Weston's millwright business is all but gone."

Minnie thought for a moment before continuing. "The Westons is black, and theys is free, but what does 'freedom' look like for them now that theys don't have a business and can't support there selves?" she asked Bridgit, not really expecting an answer. "Same goes for white folks. What does 'freedom' mean for all them white folk who now can't make a livin' and can't support theres families? They had 'freedom' before we was made 'free', but now they has nothin'," Minnie replied. "White masters like Betty-Sue's papa was always real good to us and I ain't saying slavery was right an' all, Ma'am, far from it, but now that we is free, what's gonna happen to all them good white folk? They ain't 'free'."

"I'm sorry, did you say that a *black woman* owned slaves?" asked Bridgit, still stuck on the earlier comment and not having recalled learning that in her history lessons.

"Yessum. Her husband couldn't own 'em 'cause he had once been a slave hesself and so it was against the law. Maria Weston's not the only negro to own slaves, Ma'am, although most are owned by mulatto – half-cast – rather than free blacks. But Mrs Weston's skin is as dark as mine," Minnie held out her arm and slid back her sleeve to illustrate the statement.

Black women and free former slaves all owning slaves - Bridgit was certain that never appeared in her history books! "I suppose history really is written by the victors," thought Bridgit to herself.

Minnie stopped and looked about the room as though suddenly she was being pursued or at least spied upon. "I's shouldna said nothin', ma'am," she uttered in a hushed whisper and seemed to be scanning for somewhere to hide.

For the next thirty minutes or so, Minnie helped Bridgit dress, with not a word being spoken by either woman, but with an unfinished tension in the air.

"Minnie," Bridgit put her hand on the woman's arm and looked deeply into her eyes. "I would consider it a great favour if you would please continue your story and tell me more about what it is like for you here," Bridgit said in a friendly, soothing tone.

Minnie looked at Bridgit's hand, that Bridgit then withdrew from Minnie's arm, and the woman shot Bridgit a slight smile and nod.

"The mulattoes, Ma'am," Minnie started slowly and softly. They's known about town as the 'brown elite'. They sees themselves as more white than dark. They even wrote a letter back when South Carolina left the Union saying the blood of the *white* race ran through theys veins and they would give their lives to support the whites." Minnie continued dressing Bridgit as she spoke. "They has their own private clubs; they live practic'ly next door to the white masters in fancy houses; and those same white masters buy goods from their businesses... Even the Jones Hotel - you know that place, Ma'am. The fancy hotel on Broad Street. It was owned way back by Jehu Jones, a mulatto who was born a slave but who became more wealthy than many of the whites here in Charleston - and them high-tootin' mulattoes, theys hate us black folks." Minnie elongated the word 'hate' and uttered the last comment with the first ounce of disgust Bridgit had heard from the woman since they began talking.

Minnie stopped talking long enough to finish dressing Bridgit and as there were no mirrors in the room (they had gone the way of many other valuable items in the house during the war), Minnie stood back, looked Bridgit up and down, and then said, "very pretty Ma'am. You don't need no jewels to make you sparkle," and smiled at Bridgit.

The sight of Minnie being a surrogate mirror brought Bridgit's attention to the fact that she had not seen a reflection of herself since she had arrived here in this time and place, but she did notice that her skin appeared significantly older than she knew it had been only days – or was that merely hours – before.

"Thank you, Minnie," replied Bridgit as she again placed her hand on Minnie's arm, indicating the appreciation extended to more than the dressing assistance.

As Bridgit was leaving the room, Minnie stopped her.

"Ma'am," Minnie said, getting Bridgit's attention.

"Yes, Minnie?" Bridgit replied.

"Don't get me wrong. Cap 'n' me, we is very blessed to be free, but I don't rightly know what it means for blacks like us, or for anyone else in the south, for that matter – black or white."

Bridgit smiled and tipped her head to the young woman before proceeding downstairs.

# Chapter Four - Dinner with the Enemy

"I don't understand why we are going to this dinner if you hate them so?" asked Bridgit as the two women walked from the house to the hotel where the festivities were in full swing, followed several paces behind by the ever-loyal Cap.

"I may hate them," said Betty-Sue, "but now that the war is basically over and it seems they have won, a girl needs to do what it takes to be on the winning side," she continued primping her hair and brushing her skirt as she walked. "I may look like a frightful mess, but there's bound to be a wealthy Yankee looking for a pretty young southern belle to marry - and I'll not stay in the south a moment longer than I have to now that our whole way of life is gone."

They stopped just before walking up to the door, as if mustering the courage to put on the front required to continue.

"What I don't understand," Betty-Sue said in an uncharacteristically tempered and sober tone, "is that South Carolina joined the other states to form a Union, but we never gave up our State's rights. Even when Billy McGraw entered West Point - you wouldn't remember him, he enlisted before you arrived - but he pledged allegiance as a South Carolinian, not as a member of the Union," Betty-Sue paused before continuing in a considered manner that Bridgit had not encountered in her companion prior to this conversation. "When the whole hullaballoo started, they made all those soldiers go back, and in the chapel in front of God and their commanding officers, to swear their fealty now to the Union. There was no more mention of their state in their oath, and I don't blame all our southern boys for refusing to change their oath."

Both women were silent and still for a moment, pondering what had just been said.

"They crow about fighting for the slaves' 'freedom', but what about our freedom to leave a union that no longer served us?" Betty-Sue hushed through gritted teeth.

Bridgit admitted to herself, this was an argument she had never considered – and after this pronouncement, she also wondered how much of Betty-Sue's 'southern belle' hysterics were merely an act...

"They took away our freedom to choose and in the process, they have destroyed the south, but they will not destroy me," said Betty-Sue, and added slowly with venom, "I may hate them, but I hate even more what they have done to us, stealing our way of life – our very existence – and making all Southerners basically slaves who are now dependant on the North. I have the freedom to choose any one of those eligible Yankees as a rich husband, and by God I will extract every ounce of revenge when I do."

With that, the two women entered a gay scene as the two-hundred or more passengers from the 'Oceanus' ship that had just arrived from New York were celebrating with local Union supporters – and those like Betty-Sue who had decided to abandon their principles (if they had any) and side with the victors.

Almost immediately, Betty-Sue had found moderately handsome quarry and was off batting her eyelids at every potential and suitable suitor, leaving Bridgit to stand alone beside a drape-less window.

"Are you enjoying yourself?" asked a man who, despite being stout with drooping eyes and a large forehead, had an aura of confidence about him.

"Yes, quite," replied Bridgit.

"There is no one to introduce us, so please allow me to do the honour," said the man. "Henry Ward Beecher, at your service."

"La..." Bridgit hesitated just before she was to introduce herself as Lady Bridgit Darnell but not quite sure who she was here in this time and place, she feigned a cough and started again.

"I am so sorry. Something must have caught in my throat," Bridgit excused herself. "My name is Charlotte."

"My goodness," said Beecher. "How mysterious. Just Charlotte?"

Bridgit smiled sheepishly at him and replied, "perhaps a woman needs to keep some mystery in these troubled times, sir."

"Indeed," replied Beecher with a smile, now seeming very interested in Bridgit for far more than her conversation.

Feeling uncomfortable under his glare, Bridgit reflected on his name. She had read 'Uncle Tom's Cabin' by Harriet Beecher Stowe many years ago, and wondered if there was a connection.

"Beecher is an unusual name," Bridgit started. "Are you by any chance related to the author of 'Uncle Tom's Cabin'?"

Beecher looked startled. "I would not have thought a woman of your good breeding would have read my sister's book," he replied more impressed than shocked.

Bridgit was about to reply, but a tall, slender older man approached and said, "excuse me," then addressed his attention to Beecher. "Pastor Beecher, we have people we would like to introduce you to."

Beecher smiled at Bridgit, took her hand kissed it, and bid her farewell.

Feeling out of place in the festivities, Bridgit made her way to Betty-Sue, advised her that she was going to retire to the house, but would send Cap back to escort Betty-Sue home safely.

Holding court for three men who seemed to hang on her every word, Betty-Sue simply waved Bridgit away, and that was her cue to depart.

On their way back to the house, there was barely a candle lit in the now desolate city. One of the New York passengers had even compared Charleston to Pompeii.

The passenger list on the 'Oceanus' may have only been around two-hundred, but considering the entire white population of Charleston was minimal after 1863 when the Confederate Army had urged all non-combatants to leave the city, the New York guests still enjoying themselves in the ballroom appeared to outnumber the locals.

"Cap," Bridgit spoke.

"Yessum?" Cap replied from several steps behind Bridgit.

"Will you go in search of your family now that you are free?" asked Bridgit.

The two continued on past three buildings – or what was left of them – before Cap spoke.

"I's don't have no family, Ma'am. Not other than Minnie," he replied.

"What about dreams, aspirations for your life? What do you want to do with it now you are free?" Bridgit asked, realizing she may be inciting Cap's mutiny from Betty-Sue's hold by encouraging him.

Again, pausing before he spoke, Cap replied in a deep measured tone. "You talk of freedom, Ma'am, like all of a sudden we is now able to live side-by-side with the white folks, shop where they shop, go to school and learn what they learn..." They both stopped walking.

"I has always had 'freedom', Ma'am," Cap continued. "The freedom to think what I want to think. No law or master could ever take that from me. The freedom to think and to feel love. The freedom to see God's beauty in a sunset. I has always had those freedoms. But freedom to live a different life?" Cap simply shook his lowered head and waited for Bridgit to continue toward the house.

Bridgit had been attempting to ascertain Cap's age since she first laid eyes on him, but could not decide whether he was in his thirties, his sixties, or somewhere in between.

Feeling there was a significant story – and perhaps even a philosopher – behind Cap's response but not wanting to push the issue, Brigit did not speak again until they arrived at the house and Cap stood at the bottom of the steps while Bridgit walked to the top and opened the door. Before entering, she turned to Cap and said, "It seems we are both without family, Cap. My parents are dead, I have no brothers nor sisters, everyone close to me has already passed away," Bridgit paused realising that was not technically correct given she was currently in 1865, but not wanting to be caught up by technicalities continued. "Just remember, there are things in this life that are beyond what we could possibly imagine – and if you really want something strongly enough, I believe it can come true."

Bridgit wondered how strong her belief would need to be to find a way home...

"Thank you, Ma'am," responded Cap with almost a reverence in his tone. Bridgit smiled and closed the door behind her.

Chapter Five – The Flag is Raised

The following morning, Good Friday, started earlier than most as Charleston prepared for the flag-raising ceremony over Fort Sumter where the conflict started almost to the day four years ago.

In a city that many viewed as the cradle of the rebellion, it was a strange sight to see American flags on house after house, flapping in the South Carolina breeze, as opportunistic imports from north and south alike quietly looted what was left in abandoned houses and offices.

"Excuse me, Ma'am," said Minnie in a whisper as she entered Bridgit's bedroom. Stirring, Bridgit opened her eyes and saw Minnie standing to one side as if she were waiting for something.

"Yes, Minnie?" said Bridgit in a sleepy voice.

"Ma'am, it's just that Cap and me has been able to get on a boat to go over to Fort Sumter for the flag raisin' and we was wonderin'," Minnie paused before continuing with hesitation. "We wondered whether you might like to come with us?"

Knowing the significance of the day in history, Bridgit couldn't resist the offer, even if she did wonder whether it was the sensible thing to do.

"Yes, thank you, Minnie. Please help me dress. How much time do we have?" asked Bridgit.

"The boats is leavin' at 10:00am, Ma'am," replied Minnie.

"Well, we had best get to it!" Bridgit smiled at the servant as she removed the covers and alighted from the bed.

Charleston Harbour looked like a child's bath into which they had put every possible item that could float, large and small. Steamships, flatboats and dugouts all ferrying soldiers, civilians, black and white alike to the small island at the mouth of the Harbour. Even the legendary Captain Smalls was there conveying people to the Fort. Smalls had been a black slave from Beaufort who three years earlier stole a ship, the 'Planter', from under the noses of the Confederate army and, with the help of the other slaves onboard, sailed her past the blockade and surrendered the

'Planter', her cargo, and vital military intelligence to the United States Navy - and in the process gained his freedom and a sizeable amount of money, before going on to fight for the Union army.

More than three thousand people crammed onto the tiny mound of land that housed the remains of Fort Sumter, and with Minnie on her one side and Cap on her other, Bridgit stood ready to watch history unfold.

After a song and some prayers, the telegram was read aloud that Major Robert Anderson sent on April 13th, 1861 to the United States Secretary of War Simon Cameron, informing him that, after a 34-hour-long bombardment, Anderson had surrendered the fort to Confederate General Pierre Beauregard.

As the aged-looking Anderson, now a Union General, walked to the podium, Bridgit wondered how it must have felt to surrender to Beauregard; a man who only a few years earlier had been one of his pupils at West Point. Previously, the relationship between Anderson and Beauregard had been merely facts she learned in her history lesson along with many other details about the Civil War, but now, seeing Anderson in the flesh - a Kentucky native who had been pro-slavery and a former slave-owner himself - and standing on the very site of the beginning of the conflict, Bridgit began to have an entirely different perspective - not only about this moment, but about the importance and significance of each and every moment in one's life, and how *no action nor thought is ever in isolation...* She began to feel the beginnings of a profound insight into the interconnectedness of absolutely everything…

"After four long, long years of war, I restore to its proper place this flag which floated here during peace, before the first act of this cruel Rebellion," said Anderson as three sailors attached the flag to the halyards and Sergeant Hart, the man who had lowered the flag, began to raise it once more.

Battered, tattered, shot-stained and torn, the flag that was taken down in surrender almost four years earlier to the day, was now raised in triumph - to the cheers and exultations of the crowd. As the flag unfurled, a small posy that had been wrapped inside the folded flag dropped to the ground - and for a moment, Bridgit thought she remembered something about that tiny bunch of flowers, but perhaps it was just her imagination...

As the flag reached its zenith, the roar of the crowd was drowned out by the sound of six cannons fired from Fort Sumter, followed by blasts from the various fortified batteries surrounding the harbour.

After Pastor Beecher's hour-long speech, the crowd began to disperse, again turning the harbour into a patchwork of bunting-covered floating mish-mash that looked as though one could step from vessel to vessel, all the way to land without getting one's feet wet!

Just as they were walking toward the boats, a man in his forties approached Bridgit. "Pardon, Miss, but could I take your photograph – with your two companions?" he asked, and motioned that he meant Minnie and Cap.

Not sure she wanted her photo taken, nor whether Minnie or Cap would be so inclined, she said, "thank you, but we must be off." However, seeing an expression of disappointment on Minnie's face, Bridgit hesitated.

"Do you want to have your photograph taken?" she asked Minnie, and included Cap by way of a look in his direction.

Minnie smiled and taking that as permission, "Sam Cooley's the name. United States Photographer for the Department of the South," said the man as he tipped his hat and quickly stepped behind a wooden box mounted on a tripod as though he thought he should capture the moment before she changed her mind.

That evening, Bridgit again found herself in a flurry of festivities at the Charleston Hotel where a ball, supper and even fireworks added to the celebrations. Betty-Sue as usual was flirting with several men, when attention was called to General Anderson who was about to make a toast…

"I beg you, now that you will join me in drinking to the health of … the man who, when elected President of the United States, was compelled to reach the seat of government without an escort, but a man who now could travel all over our country with millions of hands and hearts to sustain him. I give you the good, the great, the honest man, Abraham Lincoln."

...and Bridgit's heart sank as she realised the significance of the date – April 14th, 1865 – and what was happening in a theatre in Washington at that very moment...

Chapter Six - Reconciliation Dinner

The news of Lincoln's assassination spread quickly now that the telegraph lines were hastily being repaired across the land.

When reports reached Charleston, they were met with a surprising mix of sentiments and reactions. Despite Lincoln's role in the conflict that had essentially destroyed the city, Charlestonians in the seeming majority met the news with heart-wrenching wails, quiet sobs, and silent astonishment – at least publicly. Those who applauded Booth's actions may have been just as numerous, however given they largely confined their comments to private parlours, the appearance was a city who en masse mourned a departed leader.

While dining with Betty-Sue at one of the few remaining such establishments in Charleston, Bridgit was startled when she felt a hand on her shoulder. "I didn't expect to find you here," said the woman with a smile in her voice. "I thought this place had closed!"

"Anna!" gushed Betty-Sue. "We didn't think we would see you back in Charleston. How are you? How is the roof? How horrid for you!"

"One question at a time," said Anna as a waiter approached and asked Betty-Sue if she would like Anna to be seated at their table.

"Of course," said Betty-Sue to the coloured waiter in a tone that demonstrated even though the war was over, Betty-Sue nonetheless considered negroes to be her inferior. Still, in Betty-Sue's defence, she considered herself superior to most people, black or white.

Once she was settled, Anna spoke. "I am fine, the roof is a mess, and yes, it was horrid," said Anna with a sly grin that gave away her feelings toward Betty-Sue.

"What happened to your roof?" asked Bridgit, obviously not recalling this particular incident.

"It was friendly fire, I'm afraid," said Anna. She was about to continue, but Betty-Sue jumped in.

"Oh, it was dreadful! I can't believe y'all can't remember it! ...and poor Mr Roper! I kept thinking our house would be next - and with Father away, what were we supposed to do?" Betty-Sue's dramatics were past wearing on Bridgit's nerves. Now she simply accepted them, ignored them, and moved on.

"Friendly fire?" asked Bridgit in an attempt to return the conversation to a somewhat normal keel.

"Yes," replied Anna. "I was staying with the Roper Family a couple of years ago but we left long before it happened. I wasn't around to witness it myself, but in February when our troops decided that to remain and defend the city was pointless, they chose to withdraw."

"That Sherman creature should have been drowned at birth," blustered Betty-Sue in response.

"Please go on," said Bridgit, shooting a glance at Betty-Sue that suggested her interruptions were less than helpful.

"One of the canons was too large to move so, rather than leave it for the Yankees, our boys decided to blow it up, but they did the job a little too well," Anna explained. "Part of the cannon flew right over the DeSaussure and Ravenel houses, and landed in Mr Roper's roof!"

"Heavens!" replied Bridgit. "Was anyone hurt?"

"No, thank goodness," said Anna.

"But who knows how many people might have been killed, or worse, if only they had all been home when it happened," Betty-Sue continued with her histrionics.

"Killed or *worse*?" laughed Anna.

"Oh, y'all know what I mean," said Betty-Sue, now a little flushed with embarrassment.

"Anyway, I am glad I caught you," said Anna, moving the conversation along. "I was just here dining with Mr Fredericks and his niece, Maria. She is about to head to London to be married to a wealthy widower she met here in Charleston just before the war began. He and his son have already returned to England and Maria will follow as soon as suitable passage can be arranged," Anna continued. "We were discussing our invitations to the banquet Mr Nat Fuller is putting on at his restaurant."

"Invitations? We didn't get any invitations!" remarked Betty-Sue with alarm. "Why weren't we invited?"

Anna laughed a little under her breath. "Calm down," she said. "Ours only arrived today. Maybe yours is already at home waiting for you..."

Sure enough, when they arrived back at the house, two envelopes containing the said invitations were awaiting their arrival.

"One week!" screamed Betty-Sue. "How am I supposed to find something suitable to wear to a banquet and to look presentable in one week? Ooooohhhh, how I hate those Yankees," she cursed as she walked up the stairs in a huff.

When the evening finally came, it seemed Charleston's elite - black, brown and white - all turned out in the finest splendour they could muster for the event at 'The Bachelor's Retreat', a fine-dining restaurant owned and operated by former slave, Nat Fuller, that had now re-opened on Church Street.

Fuller's culinary artistry and expertise was well-known in Charleston and the Low Country, and it was with much delight that his guests took their seats and awaited the sumptuous feast, or "miscegenation banquet" as Mrs Frances Porcher called it, grumbling under her breath.

Bridgit was astonished at the sight before her. Black women sitting next to white men sitting next to brown men... All dressed in their finery, and all there with a common cause – to move Charleston forward from the repulsiveness and degradation of the war, and into an unknown future... together.

Nat Fuller took his position at the head of the room and the profound nature of this historic moment where an ex-slave is presiding over a dinner for Charleston's elite was not lost on Bridgit.

As the host, Mr Fuller invited the entire gathering to stand with him and toast to the deceased President who made this day happen, and to the independent, self-determining way of life they expected to follow. "Lincoln and Freedom!" he announced, as white and coloured alike stood side by side.

"Where did he get all this food?" exclaimed Betty-Sue.

Food in Charleston had become a scarce commodity at the end of the war. Once-prosperous planters were often forced to stand in line for rice rations. A single barrel of flour would fetch up to $250 and could rarely be found if you had the money – and even if you did have the money, no one would exchange food or anything else for Confederate dollars.

This meal, however, made it seem as though there was food a-plenty to be had for one and all, for after a choice of either Mock Turtle Soup or Oyster Soup with Celery (that itself had followed an elaborate array or hors d'oeuvres), the guests were presented with Fried Whiting, Shrimp Pie, Poached Bass, Capon Chasseur, Aged Duck with Seville Oranges, Partridge with Truffle Sauce, Venison with Currant Demi-Glace, Lamb Chops with Mint Sauce and Beef A La Mode.

After an equally elegant array of desserts, the party began to mix and mingle.

"Well, she is certainly enjoying herself," said Anna as she came to stand beside Bridgit and looked toward Betty-Sue who, as was her form, was surrounded by a flurry of potential suitors.

"I don't think I was ever that young," said Bridgit with a grin.

As she said it, the thought again came to Bridgit's mind that at this moment in

April 1865, on the other side of the ocean, and in another reality – or dimension, or universe, or whatever – she, herself, as an infant of only five-months was happily delighting both her doting mother and her adoring father. Then she felt as though her world had collapsed when she realised the month of June and her mother's untimely death was only weeks away.

"Are you all right?" asked Anna with concern, noting Bridgit's suddenly pale complexion. "Let's go outside for some fresh air," Anna continued as she took Bridgit's arm.

Bridgit wasn't sure whether the freshness of the night air helped her to collect and structure her thoughts, or just the opposite. After a long silence, Bridgit finally spoke.

"Anna, do you ever wonder whether all this is real, or just our imagination?" Bridgit asked, knowing the question would sound non-sensical to anyone who had not experienced what she had recently experienced.

Looking up at the star-lit sky, Anna replied. "My late Father, God bless his soul, used to quote Shakespeare at me, "There are more things in Heaven and Earth, Horatio, than are dreamt of in your philosophy," every time I would ponder about whether this was all there was to life."

Bridgit now looked intently at Anna as the woman continued. "He passionately believed that there was more to this life than just waking up, going through your day, going to sleep, and starting all over again," she continued. "He was not a religious man by any means, but he would quote passage and verse from the Bible and a range of other texts, telling me that there were answers in those books to questions we didn't even know to ask."

"I don't know what you mean?" asked Bridgit.

"I'm still not sure I know what I mean, either," smiled Anna, "but my Father was adamant that there was much more to life than what we can see and hear and touch."

"He was particularly fond of the works of Ralph Waldo Emerson," Anna continued. "The idea that everything is interconnected, and that thoughts are things, and that we can affect our world profoundly when we make a decision to do so."

Bridgit could almost hear Markus' words as Anna spoke.

""Once you make a decision, the universe conspires to make it happen." I think that was one of Emerson's quotes," Anna concluded.

Bridgit was on the verge of entrusting her secret to Anna when Mr Fredericks and Maria approached the pair.

"Charlotte Gordon, may I introduce my Father's good friend, Mr Benjamin Fredericks, and his niece, Maria," said Anna - and Bridgit made a mental note to remember her own last name here was Gordon.

"Oh, I am so pleased to meet you," said Maria in a pleasant tone. The attractive young brunette was in her late twenties; she was slender, refined and poised, but retaining a warmth in her manner.

"Are you enjoying your evening?" asked Bridgit.

"It has been a wonderful event and everyone has been very kind to Maria," replied Mr Fredericks, a man in his fifties who matched his niece in refinement and a dignity of presence, "but I am afraid I must lose her soon," he lamented.

"Oh, yes, of course," said Bridgit. "I heard you are off to England to be married?"

Maria beamed at the thought but quieted her delight mildly before responding. "Yes, I am to marry Dr Charles Preston..."

...and at the mention of the name, Bridgit let out a muffled yet very audible shriek.

"My goodness," said Mr Fredericks with alarm. "Are you quite all right?"

Bridgit's world seemed to lose all colour, blood rushed to her face, and she felt in fear of being swallowed whole into whatever vortex or abyss she had created when she first decided to put Markus' theory of time travel to the test.

"I'm so sorry," cried Bridgit, fighting to hold back the tears and retain some semblance of propriety. "It's just that..." how would she explain herself out of this one..? "It's just that I knew a Dr Charles Preston in St. Leonards, England," said Bridgit, hoping that would cover her tracks.

Maria looked puzzled at Bridgit's reaction, but calmed the situation a little by stating, "Your Dr Preston and mine must be two different people. I am not sure where St. Leonards is, but Charles is from London."

As Bridgit pondered this last piece of information, she almost kicked herself for not realizing that *her* Charles would only be four or five years of age in 1865, and given that to the best of her knowledge he didn't follow her down the proverbial time-travel rabbit hole, there is no possibility of him being engaged to Maria.

Sensing that she still needed to calm the mood somewhat, Maria continued. "As soon as I arrive in London, we will be married and after our honeymoon, his young son will join us. Charles thought about sending the boy off to boarding school, but I want an opportunity to be his new mother," she continued with obvious caring in her voice. "His real mother died shortly after childbirth, so he has never known a mother's love."

"That's very commendable of you," added Anna. Concerned and confused over Bridgit's reaction, Anna glanced at her before Maria continued.

"Not really," said Maria. "You see, I already love them both so much that I feel incomplete when we are not together."

"What a lovely thing to say," said Bridgit, still feeling there was more to this story, and wondering what the connection, if any, there was between Maria's Charles Preston and hers. Bridgit was struck, however, by the genuineness and sweetness to Maria's demeanour.

Maria felt for a delicate chain hanging around her neck and held forward the item that was attached to it. "Charles gave me this ring before he left. It is a family heirloom," she said as she held out the tiny ring. "I think it was his grandmother's, or perhaps great-grandmother's – how dreadful of me not to recall which," Maria continued. "He had given it to his first wife, but when she passed away, he decided to hold it safe until either he married again, or until little Charles came of age and found the woman he wanted to marry."

Bridgit went white as she saw the same posy ring Charles had given to her in England in 1895 – the ring he said his great-grandfather had given to his great-grandmother and that had been passed through the family until his father had given the ring to his beloved mother... The ring inscribed, "when this ye see, remember me." The ring Bridgit held so dear among the precious artefacts she chose to anchor her on this journey. This ring that Charles' father had given to Maria before he and *her* Charles as a young boy had set sail back to England.

Tears welled up in Bridgit's eyes and as one overflowed onto her cheek, Anna caught sight of the wayward droplet and before anyone else could notice, quickly suggested everyone return indoors to the festivities.

Taking Bridgit aside, Anna put her hand on Bridgit's arm and asked with obvious uneasiness, "are you going to tell me what is going on?"

Bridgit patted the hand of this woman who had become a good friend in a very short space of time. "Perhaps later," Bridgit said with a melancholy smile. "I think for now I just want to go home."

Chapter Seven ~ Martyrs of the Race Course

Bridgit awoke early, dressed and wandered to the shore, looking out over a now peaceful harbour that had been the focal point for both the beginning and the end of the conflict. She pondered on how Charleston had become a very surreal place in the days since the surrender. Black troops patrolled the streets. White former slave-owners were coming to terms with what life would now look like for them. Former slaves themselves were unsure of their place in this new post-slavery world.

The entire southern economy that had relied on slave labour to produce and manufacture had now ceased to exist, essentially making the south reliant on, and in many ways, subservient to the north. In time, Bridgit thought, a new type of bondage would replace that of buying and selling human beings in order to produce from the land - the bondage of sharecropping and crippling debt...

The notions of north and south were now merely points on a compass, as Private Sam Watkins of the defeated 1st Tennessee Infantry would later write - but while the nation had united, the people had not. The vernacular may have changed from 'the United States are' to 'the United States is', but that did not describe the unity or lack thereof among her people.

Bridgit's thoughts were interrupted by the echoes of cheers some way off behind her. Curious, she followed the noise until to her surprise she discovered a monumental parade of over 10,000 people at what was the former race course. During the war, the track and its infield had been turned into a makeshift prison to house Union troops, often in horrid conditions. A crude mass-grave had been established behind the grandstand for those who did not survive the disease-ridden internment.

Bridgit knew that a day or two earlier, around twenty-eight black workmen had gone to the site, and given the soldiers a proper burial. Where once the soldiers' bodies were strewn in a mass grave, now they lie in individual plots, each marked with a plain white cross. The workmen then erected a whitewashed fence around the area with an arch that read, "Martyrs of the Race Track". Bridgit knew that much, but she wasn't sure what today's parade at the racecourse was all about.

"Excuse me," said Bridgit to a woman standing near her. "What's happening?"

"We is celebratin', Miss!" said the woman in reply. "We is free, and we is celebratin' and honourin' those who done make us free," she cried with a hallelujah tone in her voice.

Charleston's Decoration Day began at 9:00am on the first day of May in 1865, when a procession of three thousand black children singing 'John Brown's Body' commenced the parade. They were followed by several hundred black women carrying wreaths and crosses, and several hundred more black men and soldiers, marching in cadence; all finally gathering around the newly-formed cemetery, and joined by other Charlestonians – black and white.

With gusto, the group sang the 'Star Spangled Banner', but it wasn't until they began singing various spirituals, that Bridgit was struck by how interesting it was that a population who was largely illiterate would know all the words to these tunes. She began to ponder the importance of oral traditions when the first of several black ministers read passages from the bible and urged the assembled crowd never to forget the sacrifice of those soldiers – black and white – who gave their lives for the acquisition of, and preservation of, freedom.

The 54th Massachusetts and the 34th and 104th U.S. Coloured Troops then performed a double-columned march around the gravesite, before the thousands in attendance dispersed throughout the race track grounds and set about enjoying picnics and companionship.

The following day, the 'Charleston Daily News' would report, "The ceremonies of the dedication of the ground where are buried two hundred and fifty-seven Union soldiers, took place in the presence of an immense gathering yesterday. Fully ten thousand persons were present, mostly of the colored population."

Bridgit was certain both Cap and Minnie must be in the crowd somewhere although as she had little to no hope of finding them among so many people, she decided to return to the house; but was surprised to find Cap already there when she arrived.

"I thought you would have been at the parade?" she responded.

"No, Ma'am," said Cap, and Bridgit knew that if she wanted more information, she was going to have to ask directly.

"Is there a reason you didn't want to go?" asked Bridgit gently.

Cap was silent for some time before he spoke. "Ma'am, I is grateful for my freedom that them soldiers fought for, but I don't think any one of them should have died."

"But surely, if they hadn't fought – and died – in the cause of freedom, then you would still be a slave," Bridgit replied, not sure if it was a statement or a question.

"That's might be so, Ma'am, but I's just not comfortable with the whole idea that these men I has never met died to give me something that I has always had," he stated. Sensing Bridgit wanted him to continue, Cap added, "My God gave me my freedom. My freedom to breathe and to think and to love is my God-given right. Men - both black and white - may have taken away my freedom to live like I choose, but I has had a good life on the whole, and certainly not one worth killing all those good young men to change it. I honour their bravery and commitment, Ma'am, but I's not comfortable that they had to die so I might be free."

Bridgit felt her throat tighten as the emotions behind Cap's speech took hold, and she realised she had been correct in her assessment of him as a philosopher, or at the very least a deep thinker.

The two stood in silence for several minutes until Cap said, "Do y'all know of the Boat-Tailed Grackle, Ma'am?"

"No, I'm not sure I do," replied Bridgit.

"That bird is what freedom means to me. It can fly and sing like other birds, but it's a smart bird and it has learned to survive no matters what challenges it finds itself in. If the little ones does fall into the water, they has learned to swim using their wings as paddles until they gets to dry land. If food is hard to come by, they has learned to eat anything and everything – even other birds if theys need to," he continued. "They know how to survive and thrive."

Bridgit look deeply at the face of this tall, proud man and wondered at the people, places and events that had shaped his outlook.

"While I's don't expect to fly like they do," Cap smiled, "being able to sing, and being able to think, and being able to rely on myself and know I can survive and thrive no matter what – that's freedom to me."

Bridgit thanked Cap for his honesty and proceeded up to her room. It seemed that the day which was still in the early afternoon had stretched on for much longer and so Bridgit decided to take a nap before gathering the courage to find out what Betty-Sue was up to.

Resting her head on the pillow, Bridgit began thinking about what had transpired over the past few days.

Cap's definition of freedom was certainly not one she had ever considered and as she fell asleep, Bridgit wondered if birds knew how lucky they are to be able to fly...

...and then...

"Wake up, sleepy head!" cried a voice at Bridgit's bedroom door. "It's Papa Cody's big day!" said the voice as its owner disappeared down the hall.

As Bridgit opened her eyes, she saw a room remarkably similar in design and décor to her own bedroom located in St Leonards On Sea, in England in 1895 that she left when she embarked on this journey.

Indeed, Bridgit had landed back in England, only now in 1908, and was about to witness the first powered flight in Great Britain – by none other than the American wild west showman, Samuel F. Cody (and whose wife, by the way, was the first woman to fly in a heavier-than-air craft)!

Once at the Army Balloon Factory in Farnborough, the rest of the group set off in search of Cody to wish him luck.

Bridgit was in somewhat of a daze as she took in the surroundings, and accidentally bumped into a man and woman who were standing nearby.

"Oh, excuse me," said Bridgit.

"It's quite all right, I..." The man trailed off as he looked at Bridgit. "It can't be..." He took several shallow breaths as the colour drained from his face. "You can't be here..." He struggled with the words, his eyes wide and his body trembling.

His terrified expression caused Bridgit to take a step back as he took a step forward.

"...but you're dead." His words were strained and barely audible. "I was with you at the end - every minute - every second I watched you breathe slower and slower - I watched as you took your very last breaths - I held you in my arms as you slipped away - I watched you *die*, Bridgit."

Bridgit stared at him. He was older than she remembered but... "Charles?"

To stay up to date with the release of future books in the Quantum Lace series, please visit the website and add your email address to the notification list:

www.QuantumLace.com

...and I would really appreciate it if you would **leave a review on Amazon!** I look forward to hearing what you think...

Acknowledgements

It is always a tricky endeavour to thank people because there is always the tendency to forget someone!

So, first of all, anyone I haven't mentioned below - **thank you!** :-)

I would like to acknowledge and thank (not in any particular order):

- The people of Charleston, South Carolina who made me feel so very welcome when I lived there. Charleston remains one of my favourite places on the planet.

- Ms. Ashley Judd, Mr Trace Adkins, and Mr Dennis Haysbert for your presentation of 'Civil War 360' that was both stimulating and challenging - and the researchers, and curators who made the documentary possible.

- Mr Stephen Fry - who has nothing to do with the content of this book other than to continually stimulate me to learn more, and to investigate far more deeply various topics that interest me - particularly ones about which I do not know enough to have an intelligent discussion and exploration of the subject. Anything and everything I watch and read of yours both inspires me, and makes me realise - in stark contrast - just how much I *haven't* done with the brains I was given! :-)

- Mr Henry Louis Gates, Jr. who, through is programs on PBS, has taught me to look at African-American history from several entirely new perspectives.

- In Romania, the Casa Capsa Café, and The Ramada Bar and Bistro in Old Town Bucharest; and in Ireland the Embassy Steakhouse, and The Mill Bar at Riverside. Thank you to all the staff who took such good care of me as I sat at your various establishments researching and writing this book – and thank you for making sure each time my wine 'evaporated' that is was replenished!

- Tom, his wife Trisha, and brother-in-law John, who have been so wonderful to me here in Ireland.

While completing the book, I leased Tom and Trisha's apartment overlooking the Garavogue River.

- The National Humanities Center in America for your thought-provoking resources and artifacts.

- All the quantum physicists, historians, authors, presenters, researchers, seekers and others who have provided (and continue to provide in many cases) me with insights, knowledge and inspiration...

- ...and everyone who loves to read and write books... You are the ones who keep Bridgit alive...

Thank you...

...and remember, if you would like me to email you when the next book is published, simply go to www.QuantumLace.com and provide me with your email address.

Well, now that Book Three is complete, it is time to curl up and dive into the research for Bridgit's next book.

Until then, sending love and smiles to all...

Bella St John

For more information on the series and contact details for the author, please visit:

www.QuantumLace.com

About the Author

Living a globe-trotting lifestyle that most people only dream about, Leigh (Bella) St John travels the world with several suitcases that her luggage concierge service picks up and delivers to her next exotic location – this book, for instance, was written in Old Town Bucharest, Romania, and in various places in Ireland.

The Quantum Lace series is a combination of many of Bella's personal loves – quantum physics; the Victorian and Edwardian eras; history in general and forgotten or little-known history in particular; and the quests and challenges

www.QuantumLace.com

- and more specifically how we view and handle them - that make us who we are...

If you look at Bella's 'Bucket List' (http://luxuriousnomad.com/bucket-list) you will see not only what she still wants to achieve, but also the incredible things she has already accomplished.

When you meet her, you instantly understand the meaning of the word "passion" - she lives & breathes it with an enthusiasm that is contagious!

For more information and/or to contact the author, please visit:

www.BellaStJohn.com

Printed in Great Britain
by Amazon